P9-CBR-415

COURAGE in TESCO

G. P. Putnam's Sons, a division of The Putnam & Grosset Group,
200 Madison Avenue, New York, NY 10016.
First American edition, 1988.
Originally published in 1987 by Hamish Hamilton Children's Books, London.
Sandcastle Books and the Sandcastle logo are trademarks belonging
to The Putnam & Grosset Group.
First Sandcastle Books edition, 1992.
Printed in Hong Kong.
Library of Congress Cataloging-in-Publication Data
Cole, Babette. Prince Cinders. Summary: A fairy grants a
small, skinny prince a change in appearance and the chance to go
to the Palace Disco.
[1. Fairy Tales] I. Title. PZ8.C667Pq 1988 [E] 87-16235
ISBN 0-399-21502-6 (HC)
5  7  9  10  8  6  4
ISBN 0-399-21882-3 (Sandcastle)
5  7  9  10  8  6  4

# Prince Cinders

## by
## Babette Cole

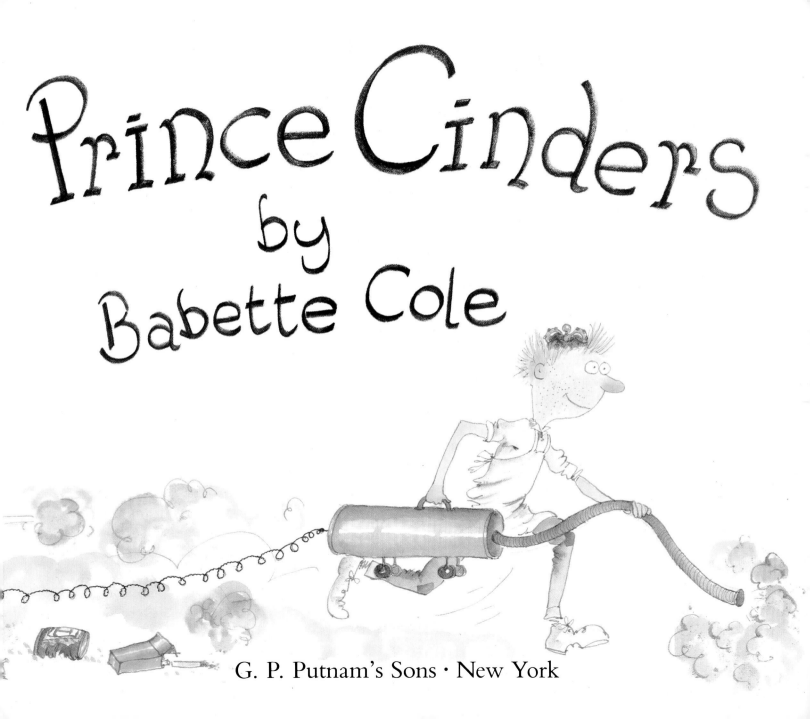

G. P. Putnam's Sons · New York

Prince Cinders was not much of a prince.
He was small, spotty, scruffy and skinny.

He had three big hairy brothers who were
always teasing him about his looks.

They spent their time going to the Palace Disco
with princess girlfriends.

They made poor Prince Cinders stay behind and clean up after them.

When his work was done, he would sit by the fire
and wish he was big and hairy like his brothers.

One Saturday night, when he was washing the socks, a dirty fairy fell down the chimney.

"All your wishes shall be granted," cried the fairy.
  "Ziz Ziz Boom, Tic Tac Ta,
  This empty can shall be a car."

"Biff Bang Bong, Bo Bo Bo,
To the disco you shall go!"

"That can't be right," said the fairy.

"Toe of rat and eye of newt,
Your rags will turn into a suit!"

"Drat!" thought the fairy.

"I didn't mean a *swim*suit!"

"Your greatest wish I'll grant to you.
You SHALL be big, and hairy too!"

Prince Cinders got big
and hairy, all right.

"Rats!" said the fairy. "Wrong again,
but I'm sure it all wears off at midnight."

Prince Cinders didn't know he was a big hairy monkey, because that's the kind of spell it was.

He thought he looked pretty good.

So off he went to the disco. The car was too
small to drive but he made the best of it.

But when he arrived at the Rock'n Royal Bash . . .

he was too big to fit through the door!

EEEEEEK!

BUS
STOP

He decided to take the bus home.
A pretty princess was waiting at the stop.

"When's the next bus?"
he grunted.

Luckily, midnight struck and Prince Cinders
changed back into himself.

DOING

BUS
STOP

The princess thought he had saved her by
frightening away the big hairy monkey.

"Wait!" she shouted, but Prince Cinders was too shy.
He even lost his trousers in the rush!

The princess was none other than the rich and beautiful Princess Lovelypenny. She put out a proclamation to find the owner of the trousers.

The Princess Lovelypenny Decrees that she will marry whoever fits the trousers lost by the prince who saved her from being eaten by the Big Hairy Monkey. Fitting sessions begin today.

P.L.

Every prince for miles around tried to
force the trousers on.

But the trousers refused to fit any of them.

Of course Prince Cinders's brothers all fought
to get into the trousers at once . . .

"Let him try," commanded
the princess, pointing at
Cinders.

"They won't fit that little squirt," sneered his brothers . . .

But they did! Princess Lovelypenny proposed immediately.

So Prince Cinders married Princess Lovelypenny
and lived in luxury, happily ever after . . .

and Princess Lovelypenny had a word with the
fairy about his big hairy brothers . . .

whom she turned into house fairies,
and they flitted around the palace
doing the housework for ever and ever.